Cooper and the Big Apple

Story by Camille Cohn

Illustrations by Riley Cohn

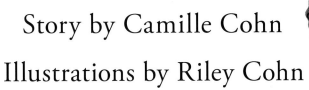

GREENLEAF
BOOK GROUP PRESS

Published by Greenleaf Book Group Press
Austin, TX
www.gbgpress.com

Distributed by Greenleaf Book Group

For ordering information or special discounts for bulk purchases, please contact
Greenleaf Book Group at PO Box 91869, Austin, TX 78709, 512.891.6100.

Design and composition by Greenleaf Book Group
Cover design by Greenleaf Book Group
Cover and interior illustrations by Riley Cohn

Cataloging in Publication Data is available.

ISBN: 978-1-62634-220-0

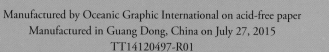

Part of the Tree Neutral® program, which offsets the number of trees consumed in the production and printing of this book by taking proactive steps, such as planting trees in direct proportion to the number of trees used: www.treeneutral.com

Manufactured by Oceanic Graphic International on acid-free paper
Manufactured in Guang Dong, China on July 27, 2015
TT14120497-R01

15 16 17 18 19 20   10 9 8 7 6 5 4 3 2 1

First Edition

For Sydney

*Thanks for being my beaming blonde
beacon of inspiration riding shotgun.*

Love, Mom

For Syd

*Thanks for being the best "big"
little sister a girl could ever have.*

Love, Ri

This is the story of Cooper. He is a little
dark grey cat who lives in a small Texas town.

Cooper likes his
life just the way it is.

One day, Cooper's best friend, Jennifer, decided that they needed to go on an adventure to New York City.

"Oh, Cooper," she said, "you will just love New York City! It is a big, amazing place filled with culture and life. Oh, and beauty and excitement, too! You will love it!"

"I love it here in Texas," Cooper thought. "Why would I want to leave?"

But that was that!

Jennifer and Cooper
headed to New York.

Cooper had never ridden on a plane before!
He ate snacks and listened to Jennifer talk
excitedly about their adventure and all the
sights they would see.

"Oh, Cooper," Jennifer exclaimed, "I am so excited for us to get to the Big Apple!"

"What apple?" Cooper wondered.
"I thought we were going to New York City."

As as the plane finally began to prepare for landing, Jennifer pointed out the window and said, "Look! There it is—the Big Apple at night. Isn't it beautiful?"

"Well, well," thought Cooper, "this isn't what I expected at all. It sure is bright!"

Jennifer and Cooper set out on their journey the
next morning. Jennifer mentioned the subway,
which made Cooper happy. He was getting hungry.

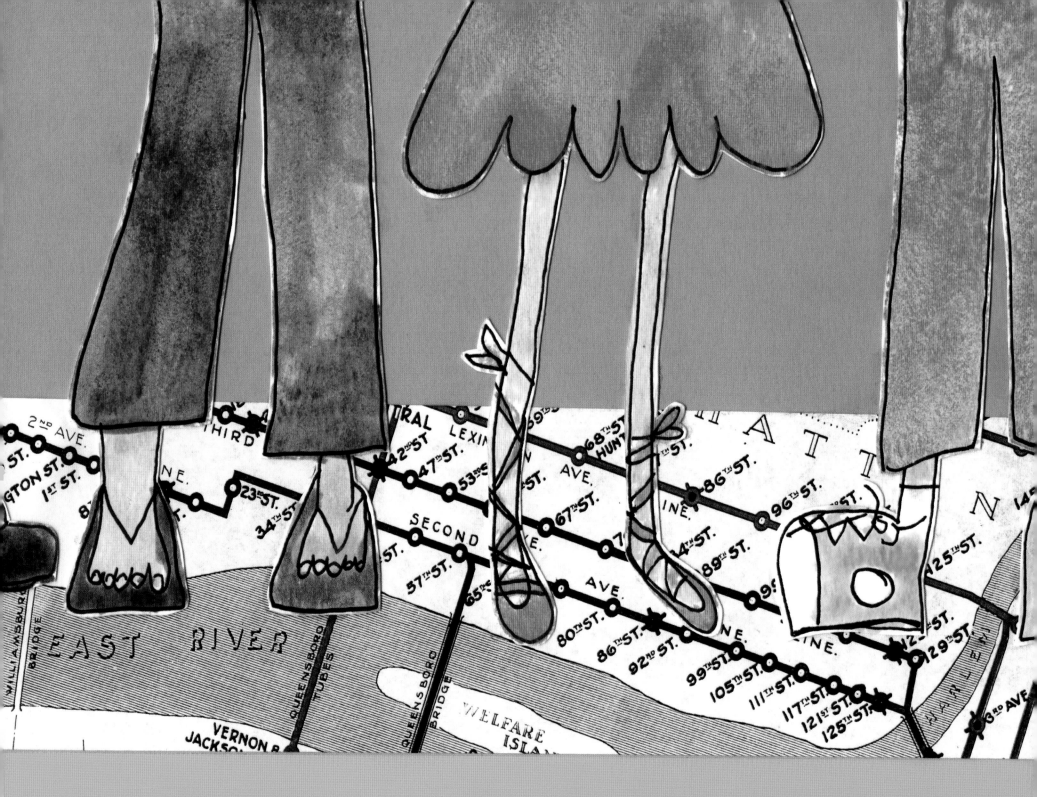

But when they arrived at the
subway station, Cooper was confused.
"Where's breakfast?" he wondered.

As they boarded the subway train, Jennifer told Cooper
they were headed to Queens to visit her friend.

"Oh my," thought Cooper, "am I dressed properly to
meet a Queen? I didn't bring my bow tie."
He was worried, but excited.

When they finally arrived, Jennifer announced,
"Here we are! This is Queens! What do you think,
Cooper?" He was confused, but relieved.

"**Well, well,**" Cooper thought.
"At least I'm not underdressed!"

After their brief visit in Queens, Jennifer
told Cooper they were going to Tiffany's.

"Oh, Cooper," Jennifer explained,
"there's a famous movie called
Breakfast at Tiffany's. It's a classic!"

Hearing "breakfast," Cooper got really
excited. "Finally, breakfast!" he thought.
He had become quite hungry since
their subway ride.

But, Cooper had
misunderstood again.

"There's not even any toast,"
he thought with a sigh.

W hen Jennifer told Cooper their next stop
was the New York Stock Market, he wondered,
"Maybe I can get something to eat there."

Jennifer was excited when they arrived.
Cooper was confused, again.

"This is not what I expected at all,"
Cooper thought. But, he remembered,
this trip had been full of surprises.

New York Stock market

"OK, Cooper," Jennifer said, "now we're on our way to Katz's deli for lunch!"

Cooper liked this idea very much. He wondered, "Could it really be . . . a deli just for cats?"

And although it wasn't exactly what he had expected, he did eat a delicious tuna salad sandwich and a cream soda, which he enjoyed very much.

"**Well, well,**" he thought, "yum!"

Jennifer told Cooper that their next stop was China Town. This frightened Cooper.

"I will have to watch where I step! I don't want to break anything!" he thought.

When they arrived in China Town, Cooper was relieved. He was also fascinated by all of the color and sounds of the interesting neighborhood.

"That was not like anything I've ever seen before," he said to himself.

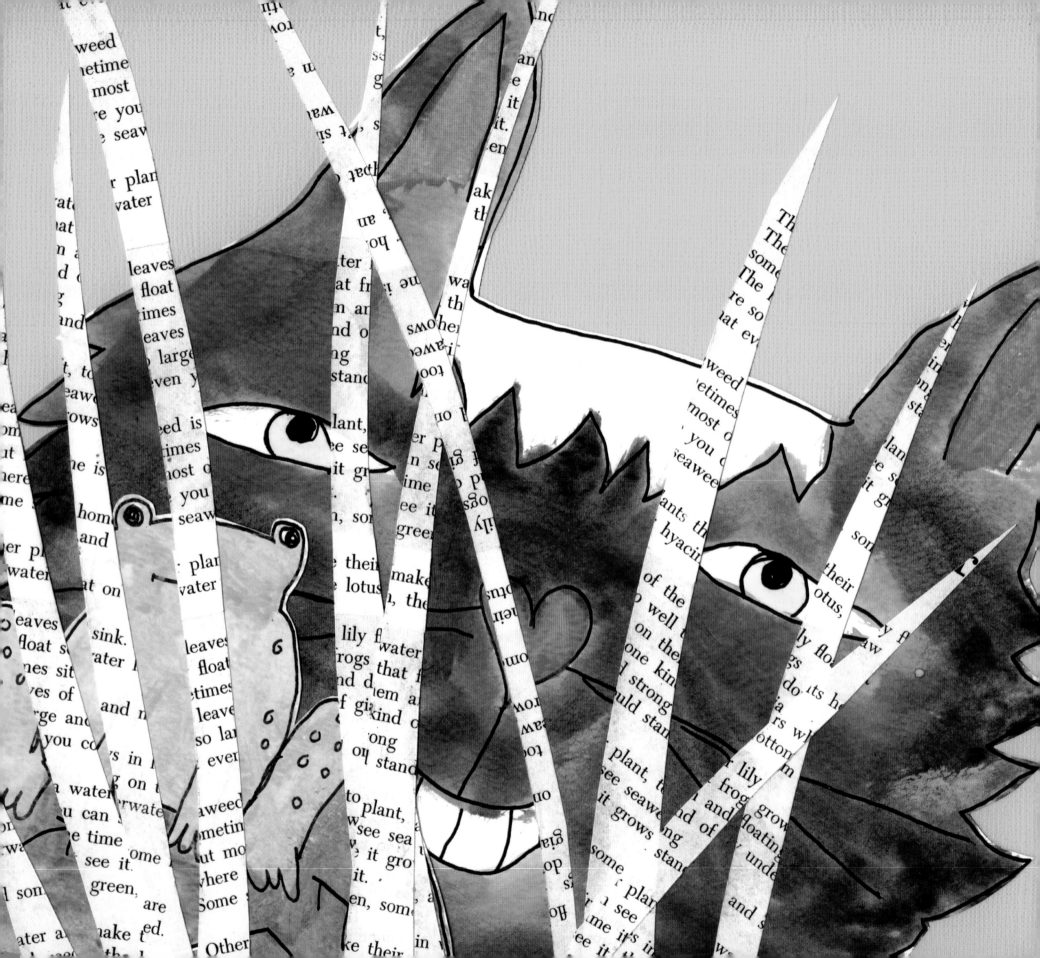

"Now we're off to see Monet's famous painting of water lilies at the Museum of Modern Art," Jennifer said excitedly. "Hurry, Cooper! Let's go!"

"Water lilies," he thought, "oh, goody!" Cooper loved a good pond. Maybe he'd even find a frog to play with.

When they arrived at the museum, Cooper was surprised, but not disappointed.

"This is much more special than playing with a frog," he thought.

"All right, Cooper," Jennifer said, as they hurried down the street, "now we're going to catch the ferry to Ellis Island and climb to the top of Lady Liberty. Let's go!"

Neither of these activities appealed to Cooper. In fact, it seemed downright rude to climb a lady!

" Well, well," Cooper thought as he gazed over the New York City skyline just as the sun began to slip below the horizon. "This is not what I expected at all. It is quite beautiful."

Jennifer told Cooper that their next stop was Times Square. How could she do that to him? She knew how much he detested practicing his times tables! Times Square sounded just plain boring.

But when they got there, Cooper was amazed at the shimmering lights and the groups of people. Times Square was really impressive and not at all what he expected.

"This is amazing!" he thought.

Cooper and Jennifer finished their evening at a Broadway show called *Cats*, which was really about cats. Then they strolled through Central Park, which was really in the center of the city.

As their taxi zipped through the streets, Cooper struggled to keep his eyes open a moment longer. In his sleepy daze, he remembered the beautiful and interesting things they had seen in New York City, but he simply could not understand how they could ever call it the city that never sleeps. He was just too tired to stay awake any longer.

"Well, well," he thought, "zzzz . . . ."

About the Author

Camille Cohn has always loved making up stories and pretending. She is currently recovering from ten years in the advertising business. When she is not herding her seven dogs or running around town (literally, especially if there's a fun run to train for), she works as a freelance graphic designer who tries not to be a helicopter mom. She lives in the Texas Hill Country with her two teenage daughters.

About the Illustrator

Riley Cohn is a sophomore at Fredericksburg High School. She lives with her mother, her sister, Sydney, and her seven dogs: Rosie, Chancho, Tooger, Schmitty, Babalou, Ouissie and Dodie. She enjoys drawing and painting, doing water Zumba, making drip castles at the beach, and swimming in the ocean when the water is really cold. Her unique perspective gives her the ability to capture a character's true essence with the simplest of strokes. Her gift of Autism gives her the ability to see the good and beauty in all.

This is Riley's second book. Her first book *Martin in the Narthex* received a Moonbeam Children's Book Award and raised money and awareness for Autism Speaks. It is available on Amazon.com.